17-
5/04
SEATTLE PUBLIC LIBRARY
D0518037
NO LONGER PROPERTY OF
SEATTLE PUBLIC LIBRARY

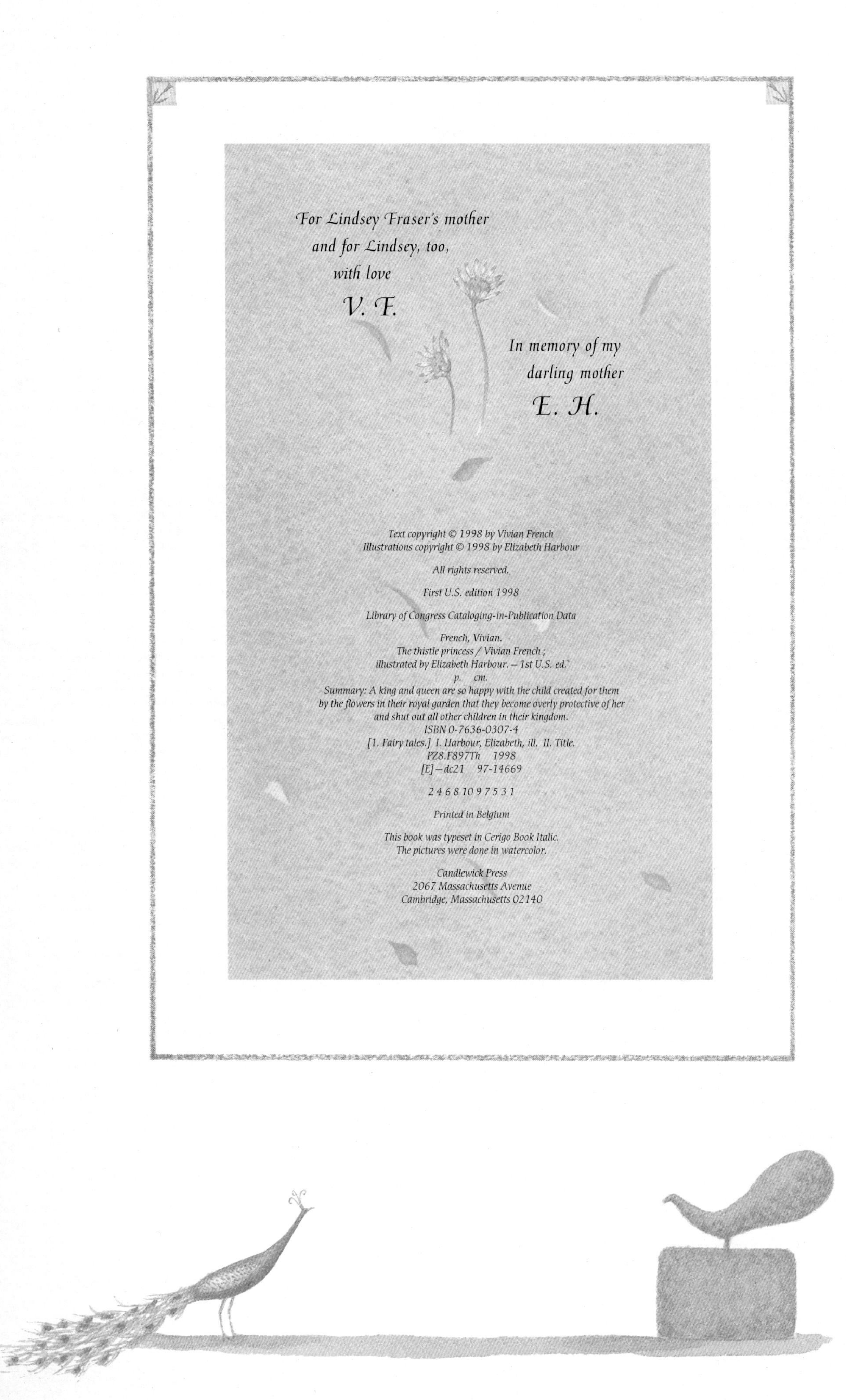

For Lindsey Fraser's mother
and for Lindsey, too,
with love

V. F.

In memory of my
darling mother

E. H.

First U.S. edition 1998

Library of Congress Cataloging-in-Publication Data

French, Vivian.
The thistle princess / Vivian French ;
illustrated by Elizabeth Harbour. — 1st U.S. ed.
p. cm.
Summary: A king and queen are so happy with the child created for them by the flowers in their royal garden that they become overly protective of her and shut out all other children in their kingdom.
ISBN 0-7636-0307-4
[1. Fairy tales.] I. Harbour, Elizabeth, ill. II. Title.
PZ8.F897Th 1998
[E]—dc21 97-14669

2 4 6 8 10 9 7 5 3 1

Printed in Belgium

This book was typeset in Cerigo Book Italic.
The pictures were done in watercolor.

Candlewick Press
2067 Massachusetts Avenue
Cambridge, Massachusetts 02140

The Thistle Princess
Vivian French
illustrated by
Elizabeth Harbour
Candlewick Press
Cambridge, Massachusetts

LONG, LONG AGO, before time was caught and kept in clocks, there lived a king and a queen. They ruled their kingdom wisely and well, but they did not smile often. Sometimes the king would look out the window and sigh, and sometimes the queen would sit under the willow tree in the royal garden and cry until the grass around her was wet with tears.

"Why is she crying?" whispered the roses.

"We don't know," murmured the lilies and poppies and daisies.

The willow shook his leafy head. "Why does the king sit and sigh?" he asked. "Who knows? Not I."

A small thistle was growing close by, hidden among the willow's arching roots.

She shook her purple head and sniffed. "How silly they are," she said to herself. "It comes of being so beautiful. They've got no sense, no sense at all. Anyone sensible could see that the king and queen want a baby, a child, a little boy or girl to run around and laugh and keep them company from daybreak to sunset. Fiddlesticks!"

And she sniffed again. If the willow heard her he took no notice. He was not in the habit of talking to thistles.

One day the gardener brought his youngest son to play in the garden.

"Excuse me for bringing him, Your Majesty," the gardener said, "but he'd like to see the flowers. He'll be no trouble."

The queen looked at the gardener's son and smiled. "He is most welcome," she said. "Everyone is welcome here."

And all day she watched the little boy as he toddled this way and that, up and down the paths, and in and out of the roses and lilies and poppies and daisies.

The king, sitting at his window, watched as well and he never sighed, not once.

"There!" said the little thistle, and she nodded to herself. "What have I been saying all along? What they need is a child of their own."

That evening, as the stars were creeping up the sky, the willow rustled his leaves.

"Ahem," he said, and the roses opened their sleepy eyes. The lilies lifted their heavy heads, and the poppies whispered, "Wake up! Wake up!" to the daisies.

"Ahem," said the willow. "I know now why the king and queen are so sad."

The flowers murmured and swayed.

"They are sad," the willow said, "because they have no children. While the gardener's child was here the queen was happy all day, and the king smiled and waved from his window."

The roses nodded. "We saw," they said. "But what can we do?"

The willow swept his long green fingers across the ground.

"There is nothing we can do. Nothing... nothing... nothing...." And he swayed and sighed, and the roses and lilies and poppies and daisies swayed and sighed with him.

The little thistle could bear it no longer. "Never mind about nothings," she said.

"What a willow is good for is baskets. Forget fancy words, old man willow—weave a fine cradle for the king and queen, and then we'll see what we can do."

There was instantly a rustling and fluttering of leaves and twigs and branches.

"A weed!" The roses trembled. "A weed telling us what to do!"

The lilies drew back in alarm, and the poppies closed up their petals tightly. The willow quivered with indignation. Only the daisies looked at the thistle with their bright eyes and nodded to her. "A child?" they asked. "Can it be done?"

"It can!" said the thistle sternly. "Now, old man willow, are you all puff and pother and words, or are you willing to help that poor lonely king and queen?"

The willow took a moment or two to decide. To be ordered around by a common thistle was a dreadful thing, but not to help the king and queen of all the kingdom was surely worse. . . .

Slowly the willow bowed his great green head, and his slender branches began to twist and weave, in and out and out and in.

"That's better," said the thistle, and she turned to the beds of flowers. "Come along! We need help from all of you."

As the willow laid the green leafy cradle on the grass, the roses leaned gently over it and dropped pink and white and deep crimson petals inside. The lilies gave their golden fragrance, the poppies their crumpled scarlet silk, and the daisies shook in a scatter of bright whiteness.

"H'mph!" The willow turned to the thistle. "I hope you have no intention of adding your sharp needles and pins!"

The thistle sighed. "There has to be more than pretty leaves and petals," she said.

The little thistle waited until the flowers slept and the night was still. Then, slowly and painfully, she pulled up her roots from the warm earth and lay down in the willow cradle. She could feel herself wilting and shriveling as she sank into the soft petals. Her strong gray-green leaves withered and grew brittle, and her fine purple head turned to silver white.

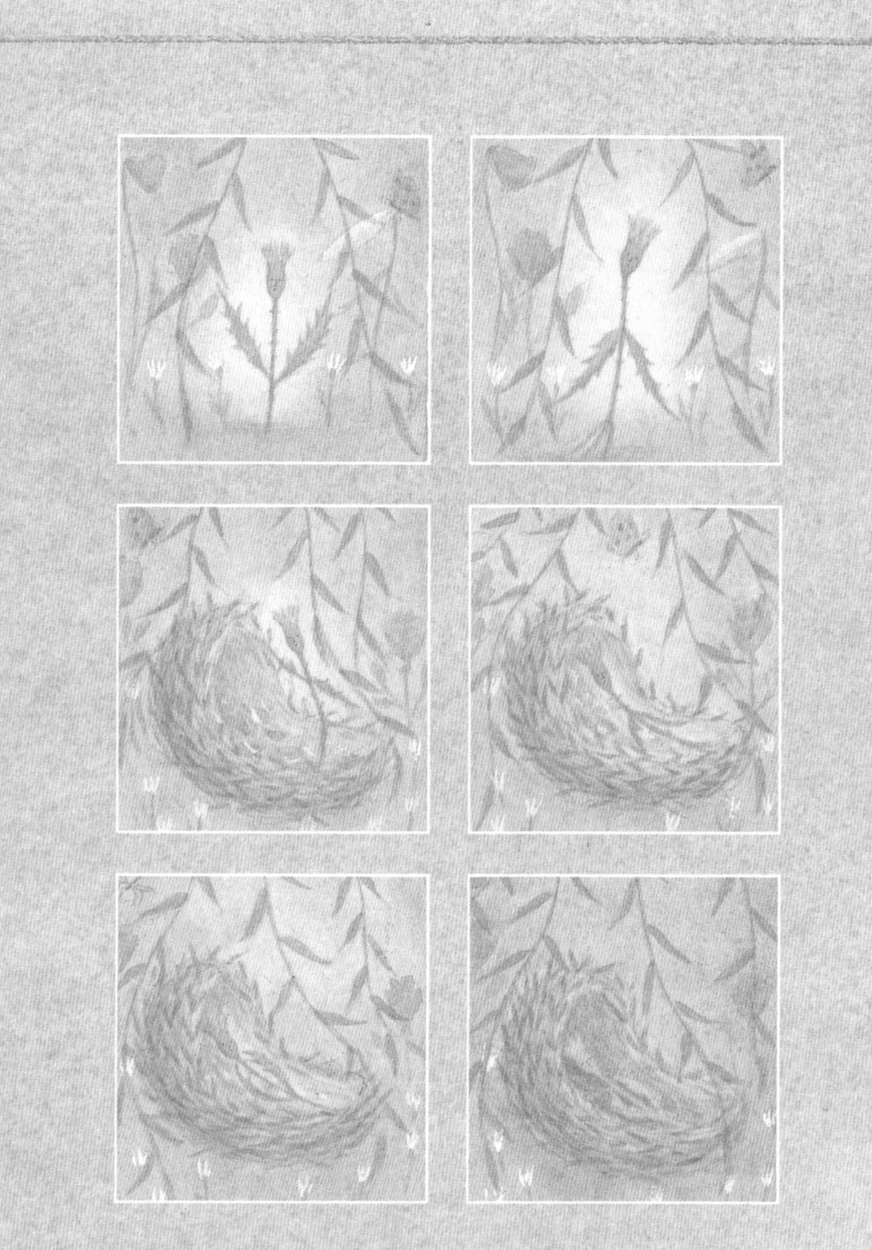

"What needs doing must be done," she said,
and never spoke again.

The willow was woken in the morning by a strange sound. It was coming from the cradle, and he peered in amazement through his long green fingers. There, lying in the basket of his own making, was a baby— a baby with the skin of rose petals and the sweetness of lilies, and bright eyes that shone as she gazed up into the leaves above. She was wrapped in scarlet silk, and she kicked her little fat legs and laughed.

The queen was the next to hear the baby. She came running down the path, her arms outstretched. The king was close behind. Together they lifted the baby from the cradle and hugged her and loved her.

"Our very own baby!" whispered the queen.

"Our own princess!" The king smiled.

"There!" said the willow to the roses and lilies and poppies and daisies. "See how happy they are?" And he rustled his leaves proudly.

The king and queen carried the baby tenderly into the palace.

"Now that we have our hearts' desire," said the queen, "we must keep her safe from harm."

"Indeed we must!" said the king, and he gave orders that a fence be built around the royal garden to keep the baby princess safe. The baby waved her little arms and cried, but the king and queen took no notice.

Children came to stare at the fence. Then the gardener's little boy wriggled in between the bars and the other children followed him. They danced and sang to the baby princess, and she clapped her hands and laughed.

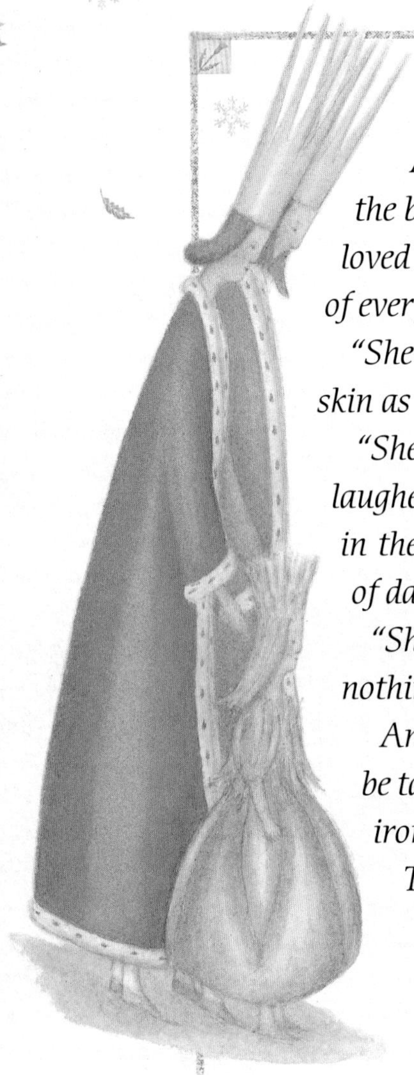

Autumns and winters came and went, and the baby grew into a little girl. The king and queen loved her so dearly that they spent every second of every minute of every hour watching over her.

"She is so beautiful!" The queen smiled. "She has skin as soft as rose petals!"

"She smells as sweet as the golden lilies!" The king laughed. "And her eyes are as lovely as the darkness in the hearts of poppies, and as bright as the eyes of daisies!"

"She is our hearts' delight," said the queen, "and nothing and nobody must ever hurt her."

And she and the king gave orders that the fence be taken down and replaced by a high wall with an iron gate.

The princess ran to the gate and pulled at it.

"No!" she called. "No!"

But the king ordered that the wall stay.

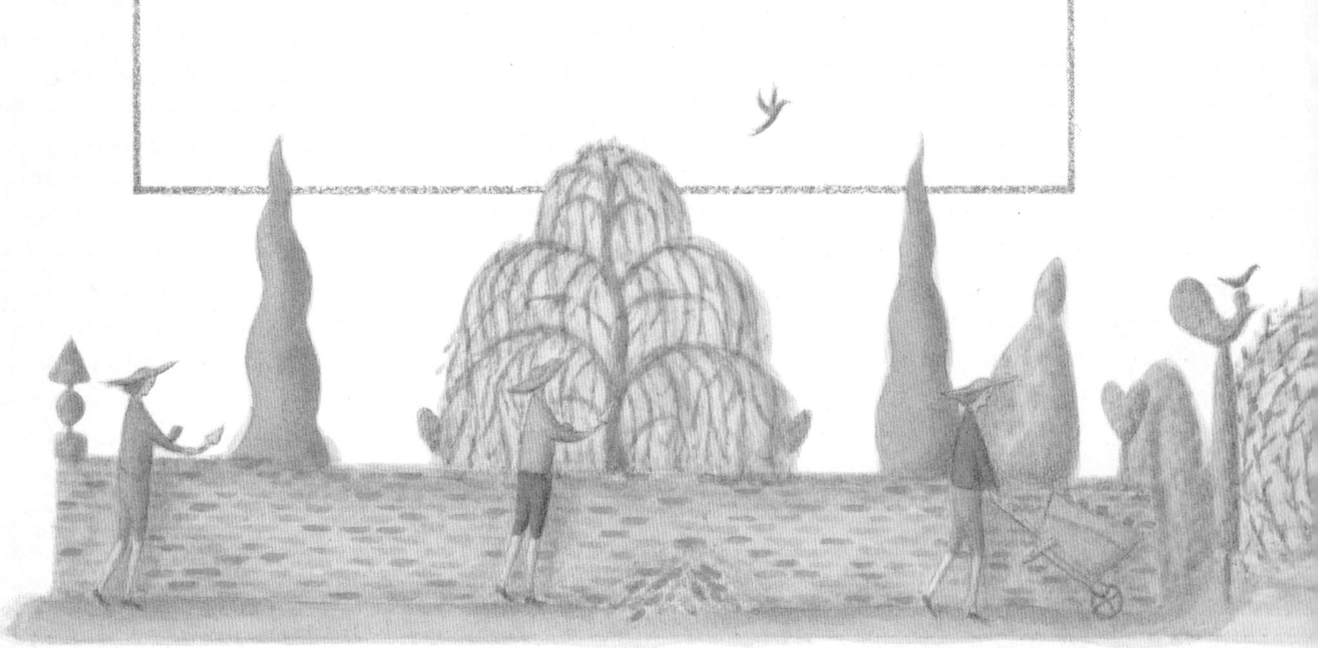

The children waved to the princess through the gate. Then the gardener's youngest son showed them how to climb on one another's backs all the way up to the top of the wall, and they hopped down into the garden.

The children played hide-and-seek and catch-as-catch-can with the princess, and she skipped and jumped and ran with them all day and every day.

Springs and summers came and went. The princess went on growing, and the garden grew too. More and more flowers sprang up and flourished, and the royal garden became the wonder of the land.

The princess and the gardener's boy walked hand in hand under the arches of pink and white and deep crimson roses, and whispered with the other children among the golden lilies. The poppies dropped their scarlet petals, and the daisies nodded and looked on with their bright eyes. The king and queen watched the princess and the children playing together and they shook their heads.

"Our daughter is so precious. What if she catches a cold, a mump, or a measle from the outside children? We must protect her from all danger."

Orders were given to build another, higher wall. Iron spikes were placed on the top, and the gates were protected with the strongest steel bars.

"Please let my friends come in," begged the princess. "Please let them come and play!"

But the king and queen only patted her and smiled fondly at her.

"Sit with me under the willow," said the queen, "and I will sing to you."

"Walk with me in the garden," invited the king, "and I will tell you stories of long ago."

The princess looked at them. "No," she said. "No." And she went to sit curled up in the branches of the willow, and slow silver tears ran down her cheeks.

The king and queen sighed, but they told each other it was all for the best.

"Could we ever forgive ourselves if she came to any harm?" asked the king.

"She is our everything," said the queen.

Outside the children gathered around the gates, but the guards ordered them to go home.

The gardener's youngest son struggled to climb the wall, but it was too high.

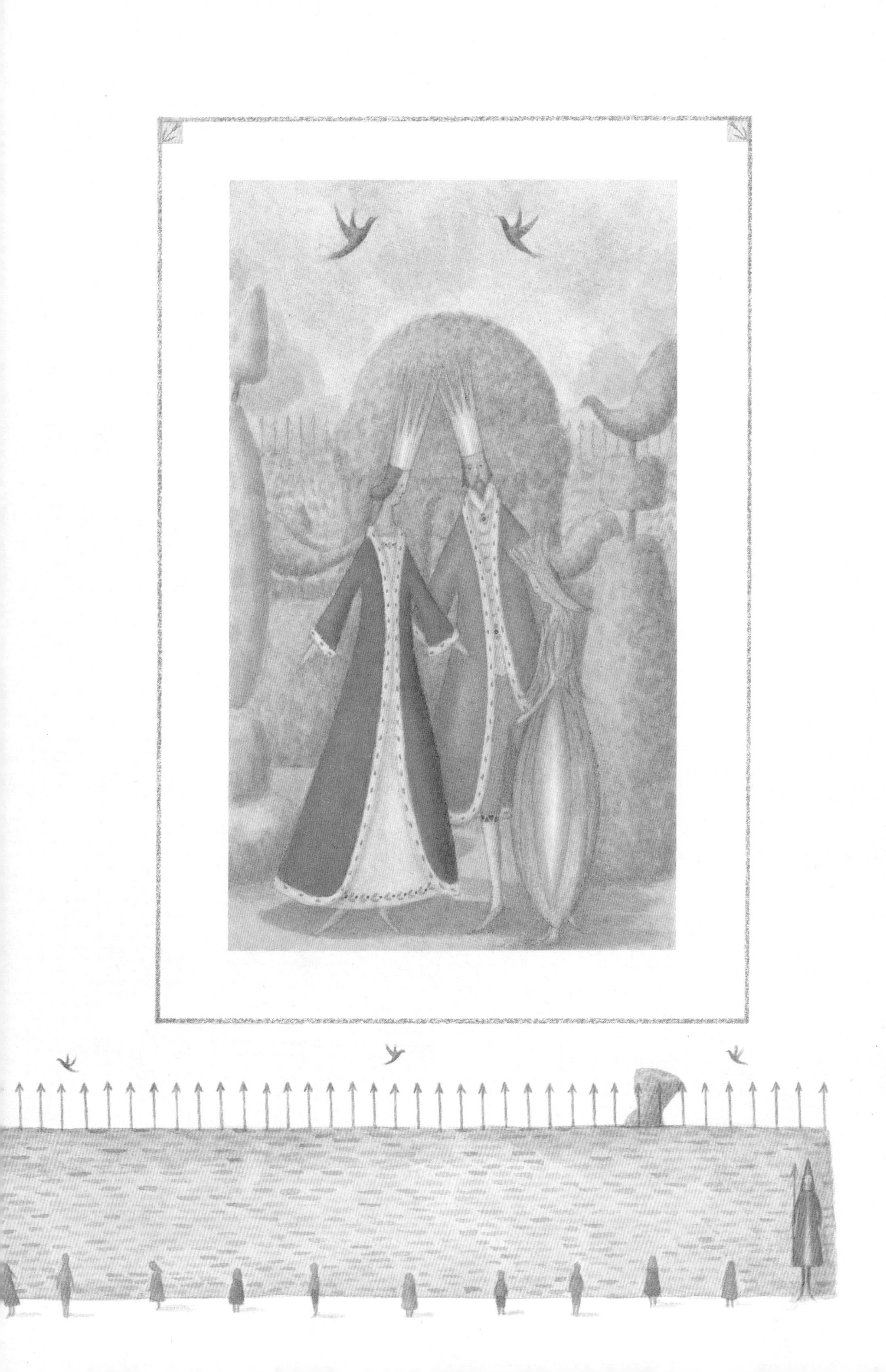

Suns and moons rose and set, and the princess grew tall and thin. She was pale now and spent most of her days sitting beneath the willow tree, listening to the murmuring of the leaves.

"How right we were to keep those noisy children out of our garden," said the queen.

"Indeed," said the king. "They were far too rough. See how delicate and tender our princess is. She is safe here in our beautiful garden. We must make it as lovely as we can to give her pleasure."

Orchards were planted, full of sweet russet apples and velvet-skinned peaches and dusky plums. Fountains sparkled and waterfalls tumbled, and in the branches of the trees gold and silver birds fluttered their shining wings. The princess grew still more pale and sad. Sometimes she walked among the roses and lilies and poppies and daisies and sighed, and sometimes she sat under the willow tree and cried until the ground was wet with tears.

Outside the walls the children lived their lives, but they seldom laughed or danced or sang. The gardener's youngest son often sat outside the gates, and one or another of the children would come and sit with him. They would speak quietly of the time long ago when they had played in the garden.

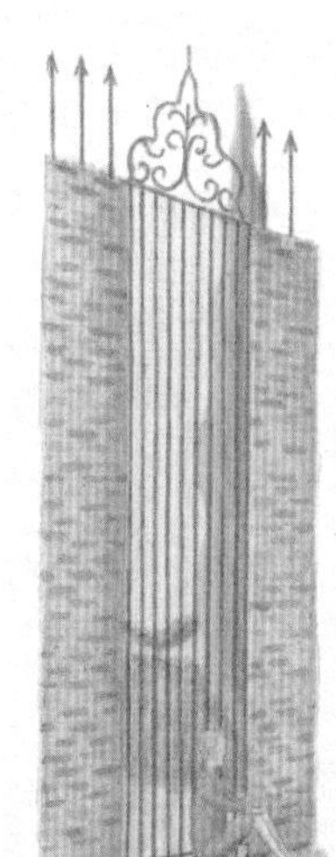

The king and queen walked under the trees with the princess.

"Look at the wonderful fountains!" the queen said.

"My friends would love to splash in the sparkling water," said the princess.

"No, no!" said the king. "Listen to the birds!"

"My friends would love to see them fly with their gold and silver wings," said the princess.

"No, no!" said the queen. The princess sighed and was silent. The king suddenly stopped.

"Look!" he said, and he pointed an angry finger. "Look! In our beautiful garden! A weed!"

"What is it?" The queen hurried to see. "Is it harmful? Will it hurt our darling?"

"It's a thistle," said the king. "Call for the gardeners! At once!"

The gardeners were called for. The thistle was taken away, but soon there was another, and then another. Professors and experts came from far and wide to give their opinion, but whatever they suggested, it seemed that there were always more thistles. Thistles grew among the roses and lilies; they grew among the poppies and daisies; and every day there were more and more and more.

"Whatever shall we do?" asked the king. "Our beautiful garden will soon be filled with thistles!"

At the steel-barred gate the gardener's youngest son was pleading with the guards.

"Let us in!" he begged. "Let us in, and we will pick the thistles. We ask no reward. Only let us into the garden and all the thistles will be gone."

The king and queen looked up at each other.
"Did you hear?" asked the king.
The queen nodded.
"Children have bright eyes," said the king. "They will spy out even the smallest thistles. They can see things we cannot."
"That is true," said the queen, and she looked toward the willow tree. The princess was curled up in the branches, fast asleep.
She's as light as down, the old willow thought, as light as thistledown.
The queen sighed.
"Our darling is so pale and sad. Maybe if the children pick the thistles she will smile again."

The king stood up.
"Open the gates!"

As the gates opened, the children came dancing in. They skipped and hopped and ran all over the garden, picking every thistle they found. They skipped among the roses and lilies and poppies and daisies, and they picked big thistles and little thistles.

They hopped among the apple trees and peaches and plums, and they picked tall thistles and small thistles. They laughed as they ran in and out and round about the royal garden, and the king and queen smiled as they watched them.

"They look so happy," said the queen. "And look, the thistles are almost gone! And no more are growing!"

The king stroked his beard. "Perhaps," he said slowly, "perhaps we were wrong to build the wall. How long is it since we heard laughter in the garden?"

The queen didn't answer. She had run to help a very small boy who had fallen among the poppies.

As she picked him up he turned to her. "Thank you," he said and he kissed her.

The queen's eyes filled with tears. "Oh," she said. "Oh — and we shut them out."

The king shook his head. "We were wrong. Our princess is our hearts' delight, but these are our children, too. The children of our kingdom."

The queen put her hand on the king's shoulder. "How wise," she said. "We must order that the wall be pulled down."

The gardener's youngest son came walking toward the king and queen, and bowed.

"If you please," he said, "there are no more thistles. Do you wish us to leave now?"

The queen curtsied. "No," she said, "we would be honored if you would stay."

The king turned to the guards. "As soon as you can," he ordered, "pull down the wall!"

The children cheered and laughed and threw their hats in the air and danced hand in hand round and round the king and queen. "Hurrah!" they shouted.

The gardener's son bowed once more. "And now," he said, "may we play with the princess?"

"Run to the willow and tell her that you may," said the queen, and the children ran with outstretched arms.

"Princess!" they called from under the tree. Up in the willow's branches the princess stirred in her sleep. "Come and play, Princess! We can play in the garden!"

"At last," whispered the princess.

Slowly she floated upward, up and up through the whispering leaves. "Princess!" the children called again. "Where are you? Where are you?"

The gardener's son rubbed his eyes. Had he truly seen the princess drifting away into the evening shadows? He rubbed his eyes again and said nothing.

The king and queen ran to the tree and stared and stared up into the branches. There was nothing to be seen and nothing to be heard, except for the soft whispering and rustling of the leaves. The waiting children looked at them expectantly. "Is she still asleep?" "Is she playing hide-and-seek?"

The king shook his head. "We found her under the willow tree when she was a baby," he said sadly, "and now she has gone."

The queen put out her hand. "You are our children," she said.

"Now and for ever and ever," said the king.

As the shadows grew longer, the old willow sighed.
"Willows weave beautiful cradles, but
I will never weave again."

A very small thistle
growing under the willow's roots
sniffed loudly. "Fiddlesticks!" she said.